Enid Blyton ™

The Smelly Little Dog

Illustrated by Pam Storey

The children rushed down on to the beach with their spades and buckets and boats. Mummy followed with the packets of sandwiches and a big bottle of lemonade. She signalled to the man who hired out deckchairs and he came hurrying up with one at once.

"There!" said Mummy, sitting down thankfully, for it was a long walk from their boarding house to the beach. "Now you've got a whole day to play and paddle and swim, children. It's so hot today that you can get as wet as you like – the sun will soon dry you."

Joan, Fred and Betsy felt very happy. The things they would do! "Build an enormous castle with a moat round it full of water!" said Fred.

"And sail my boat on those little waves," said Joan.

"And take my teddy paddling with me," said little Betsy.

"And have ice-creams when the ice-cream man comes round!" said Mummy, laughing. "Oh, here's that little dog again! Go away, dog – you're smelly!"

"Mummy, he's quite a nice little dog," said Fred. "I know he looks very dirty, though he does go splashing in the sea quite a lot and ought to be quite clean by now! And I'm sure his master doesn't give him enough to eat. He's so thin!"

"Get away from those packets of sandwiches, Dog," said Mummy crossly, as the dog came sniffing round. "You're always hungry. Why doesn't your master feed you properly?"

The deckchair man stood nearby. He chased the little dog away. "Off with you! You don't belong to anyone, do you? You're a nasty little stray!"

"He's not nasty," said Betsy, at once. "He's got a nice face. I like him. I want him to play with me."

So the little dog played with them all the morning, though Mummy shooed him away as soon as he came near her and the sandwiches.

Betsy shared her sandwiches with him when dinner-time came and so did Fred and Joan. He seemed very, very hungry, but he was quite polite and didn't snap at all. He seemed to like Betsy best and she cuddled him to her when she had finished her sandwiches.

"Betsy! You are NOT to cuddle that smelly little dog!" said Mummy sharply. "Oh, I know he's friendly enough, but it's only your sandwiches he's after. Push him away. Go home, Dog, go home!"

The little dog ran off and sat down, looking very sad. Nobody ever wanted him. He really was dirty and smelly and very thin. He would certainly have gone home if he could – but he hadn't had a home since he

was a puppy and had been left behind on the beach by a man who didn't want him. So how could he go home?

"Now," said Mummy, when all the biscuits and apples she had brought had been eaten, "you can go and buy a big ice-cream each from the ice-cream man up on the front, and bars of chocolate from the sweet shop. Take Fred's hand, Betsy."

The little dog went with them. He liked these children. They didn't throw stones at him and call him horrid names as some children did.

Perhaps he might have a lick at an ice-cream – the ice-cream man sometimes spilt some as he slapped it between the wafers.

When the children came back to the beach, their mother was fast asleep. "What shall we do?" asked Fred. "I think I'll go for a swim. Come on, Joanie."

Betsy looked sad. She couldn't swim like the others. "I shall paddle," she said. "And I shall take my teddy bear, too. He told me yesterday that he likes paddling."

"The things that bear says to you!" said Joan, laughing. "I shouldn't take him paddling, Betsy. He won't like getting his feet wet."

"He told me he did like it," said Betsy seriously. "He told me his feet were hot, like mine, and he wanted to feel the cold sea on them."

The others laughed and ran into the sea at top speed, plunging into the big waves. They were good swimmers. Betsy stood and watched them. "I can't swim, Teddy, and you can't either," she said. "But one day we'll be big enough!"

She walked her big bear down the sands to the edge of the waves, talking to him. The sea felt lovely and cool over her toes. She dabbled the bear's toes in too.

The little dog came and sat down at the edge of the sea and watched. He was afraid to go too near Betsy and the bear in case they didn't want

him. He saw Joan and Fred quite far out and gave a little bark as if to say, "Be careful now!"

But they were such good swimmers that they were quite safe. They were racing one another to the pier. Betsy watched them. "Let's go in a bit further, Teddy," she said, feeling very brave. "You're not afraid of the big waves, are you? I'm not either!"

So they went further in, the teddy bear getting wet right up to his neck! "Do you like it, Teddy?" said Betsy. "Yes, you do! Oh, look at this great big wave coming – hold my hand tight!"

The wave was really very big indeed. It curled

over just as it reached Betsy and splashed right over her head. She sat down very suddenly indeed and let go of the bear's paw. In a trice the wave had taken him away from her into deeper water! There he went, turning over and over, his little brown body as wet as could be!

"Teddy! Come back! You'll be drowned!" shouted Betsy, getting up and wading after him. But, oh dear, another big wave came and over she went again. Then, before she could get up, spluttering and frightened,

another one broke right over her and she disappeared under the water.
The wave rolled her over into the sea when it ran back on itself, and poor
little Betsy couldn't even stand up!

Fred and Joan didn't see. They were too far away. Mummy didn't see
either, because she was fast asleep. Nobody saw – except the smelly little

dog. He stood up at once when he heard Betsy scream. Then he plunged into the waves and swam steadily out to her.

And at that very moment Mummy woke up! She sat up to see where the children were – and saw poor little Betsy being taken away by the waves! She screamed loudly and began to run down the beach.

The little dog was almost up to Betsy. Ah – there she was! He snapped at her t-shirt and got it between his teeth. Then he tried to swim towards the beach with her.

But she was very heavy for such a little dog. He panted and puffed, swallowing water – but he didn't let go of the t-shirt! No – he clung on to it for all he was worth! This was the little girl who always spoke kindly to him! She was in trouble, and there wasn't anyone but him to help her.

He dragged poor Betsy into shallower water and then, just as he thought he simply couldn't hold on any longer, someone caught hold of Betsy and lifted her up.

It was her mother, who had waded out to her and the little dog! She waded back with Betsy, who was choking and spluttering and crying with fright. The little dog followed and sat down at a safe distance to watch.

"Darling! You shouldn't have gone out so far!" said Mummy, cuddling poor frightened Betsy. "You might have been drowned! You would have been if that smelly little dog hadn't gone after you and tried to bring you back!"

"I went after my teddy," said Betsy, crying. "He's still out there, Mummy. He'll drown. Oh, please get him for me!"

"I can't bother about your teddy now," said Mummy, hugging her. "I'm only too glad you are safe!"

But someone bothered about her teddy, who was now so soaked with water that he was almost sinking! Only his little bear-nose could be seen!

The little dog caught hold of him and swam back at once. He laid the bear down on the sand beside Betsy and then, as Fred and Joan came racing out of the water to find out what was happening, he went a little way away and sat down again. He was very, very glad he had been able to save the bear too, but he was sad to hear Betsy crying.

She stopped when she saw her teddy bear beside her. She took him up, soaking wet as he was and hugged him to her. "That little dog saved you too," she said. "Mummy, isn't he a good little dog?"

"Very, very good," said Mummy, hugging Betsy again. "Fred, Joan – little Betsy was nearly drowned when she took her teddy into the water for a paddle. If it hadn't been for that little dog, who raced after her and got her out of the waves, she would have been drowned. Oh, Betsy – to think I was asleep, too, and didn't know till almost too late!"

"Oh, you good little dog!" said Fred, turning to where the little creature sat, his head on one side, listening. He was very, very wet, but he didn't mind that at all. He was so very glad that the little girl he liked was smiling again.

"Mummy – I want to hug that little dog," said Betsy. "Come here, Dog, come here!" He ran up, his tail down, wondering if he was going to be scolded. But no – of course he wasn't! Betsy hugged him, Fred hugged him, and Joan too. And then Mummy patted him and spoke to him kindly.

17

"Little dog – you need a home. Would you like to come and live with us? We have an old kennel that you could have. I shall never, never forget what you did today, never! You are the best little dog in the world!"

Well, the little dog couldn't believe his ears! He licked Mummy, he pranced round, and his tail wagged so fast that it could hardly be seen. Then he went and lay down beside Betsy, his head on her knee, as if to say, "I'm your dog. I belong to you!"

Betsy understood, of course. "Yes, you're my dog," she said. "I'll certainly share you with the others, but you belong to me. And I'm going to call you Splash because you splashed into the water to save me!"

And that was how Splash came to live with a little family of his own. You wouldn't know him now! He is spotlessly clean, gleaming brown and white, his tail is always up and he is quite plump!

I know all about him because one day I heard Betsy shouting "Splash! Splash!" when she called him to her. I asked her why he had such a strange name and, when she told me, I thought I really must tell you – and that is how this story came to be written!